Published by
Peter Haddock Publishing,
United Kingdom.

Bedtime Tales

CONTENTS

Jack and The Beanstalk

9

Jack and The Beanstalk

Long ago, in a tiny village, lived a boy called Jack. He and his mother were poor and one by one their animals died until there was only one old cow left.

"Jack, take the cow to market and sell her for a good price," said his mother. "She is too old to produce milk and we need the money for food."

Jack set off for market and met an old man resting by the road.

"On the way to market, are you?" he asked.

"Yes," said Jack. "I must sell my cow."

"I'll take the cow in exchange for these magic beans," said the man. "Plant them in your garden and amazing things will happen. You'll see!"

The magic beans sounded exciting so Jack gave the cow to the man and took the beans home.

"You stupid boy!" cried his mother tearfully. "These beans won't grow! Now we shall starve!"

She threw the beans out of the window and Jack went to bed hungry and unhappy.

Next morning he opened the door and gasped as he saw a huge beanstalk reaching up to the sky.

"I wonder how high this beanstalk goes," thought Jack and he began to climb.

All day long, Jack climbed. When he reached the top it was dark. A road stretched ahead of him and he followed it until he came to a huge castle. He knocked on the door and a woman answered.

"I'm tired and hungry," said Jack. "May I rest here and have some food?"

"You may have some food," said the woman, "but, when my husband, the giant, comes home, run for your life. He eats little boys like you."

The woman ushered him into a huge kitchen and he had a delicious meal. Suddenly he heard the thunder of giant footsteps and hid in a big copper pot. The giant came in and roared,

"Fee, fi, fo fum,
I smell the blood of an Englishman!"

"Nonsense, dear," insisted his wife. "Your hunger is making you imagine things."

He ate his meal noisily and then bellowed,

"Wife! Bring me my money!"

Jack carefully lifted the lid of the pot and saw the giant's wife stagger in, carrying several bags of gold. The giant emptied the gold on to the table and began to count it while his wife went to bed.

When he had finished, he put the coins back in the bags, laid his head on his arms and went to sleep. Silently, Jack climbed out of his pot, crept up to the table and took three bags of gold. Then he slipped out of the castle and back down the beanstalk.

Jack and his mother had enough gold to keep them living comfortably for the rest of their lives and Jack should have settled down but he was restless, so, one morning, he climbed the beanstalk again and headed straight for the castle where the giant's wife answered the door.

"You must not come in!" she cried. "My husband will find you and eat you for sure!"

But Jack looked so tired that she let him in for a meal. He had hardly finished eating when he heard the giant's roar and ran to hide.

"Fee, fi, fo fum,
I smell the blood of an Englishman!"

"Don't be silly, dear," his wife spoke gently. "It's only the sausages for supper you can smell."

After eating his supper he called,

"Wife! Bring me my hen!"

She brought it to him and bade him goodnight and the giant roared at the hen,

"Lay, hen, lay!"

The hen laid a shining, golden egg on the table and carried on laying until there was a huge pile of golden eggs. Then the giant dozed off to sleep.

Jack sneaked up to the table, grabbed the hen, holding her beak to keep her quiet, and ran out.

When Jack reached home he gave the hen to his mother. They would now be very wealthy.

Jack's mother was very afraid, however.

"Jack," she said. "One day your father went to market and never came back. A travelling man came and told me that they had found the giant's castle and the giant ate your father up. Jack, this must be the giant you have been stealing from! Please don't go back!"

But Jack would not listen and vowed to avenge his father's death.

The giant's wife was terrified when she saw him again but, at last, let him in although he had no time to eat before the giant returned.

"*Fee, fi, fo fum,*
    I smell the blood of an Englishman!"
She calmed the giant down again and gave him his dinner. When he had finished he bellowed,
    "Wife! Bring me my golden harp!"

"Play, harp, play!" the giant commanded.

With song after song the harp entertained the giant until he commanded it to stop. When he slept, Jack snatched the harp but it cried out,

"Help, master, help!" and the giant woke up.

"Fee, fi, fo fum!

I shall eat you. Come to me, come!"

Jack, carrying the screeching harp, ran to the beanstalk with the giant lumbering after him. Jack slithered to the bottom, ran indoors and grabbed his axe. He swung the axe and chopped at the beanstalk until it broke.

"That is for my father!" shouted Jack as the giant fell to the ground with a tremendous crash.

Jack's adventures were over and he and his mother had no need to fear the giant ever again.

Cinderella

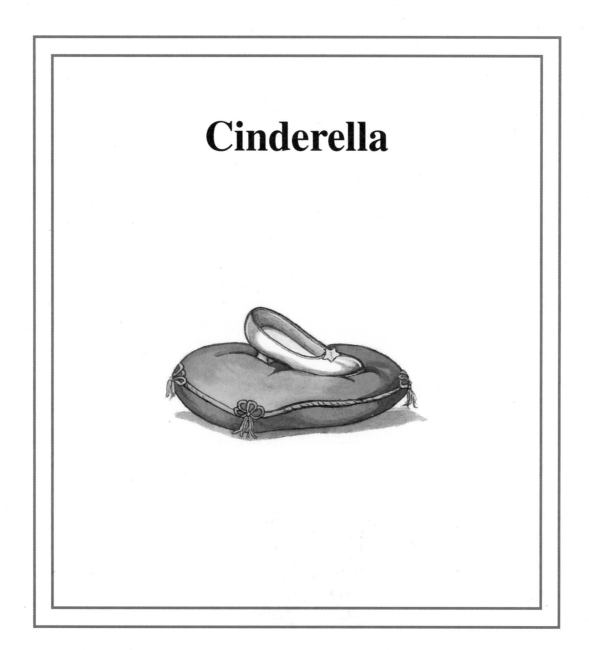

Cinderella

Once upon a time there was a young girl called Cinderella. She lived with her step-mother and two step-sisters. They were very unkind to her and ordered her about from morning until night.

"Cinderella, make the beds. Cinderella, scrub the floor."

Cinderella did all these jobs without complaining. She was a lovely girl and her ugly and bad-tempered step-sisters were very jealous of her.

Cinderella did not have a bed to sleep on; she spent the night on the hearth in the cinders. Her step-sisters had called her Cinderella because she was always covered in cinders.

One day a messenger called at the house with an invitation to a Grand Ball which the Prince was holding at the Palace.

The step-sisters' tempers were even worse than usual as they ordered Cinderella to get their fine dresses ready.

'All the handsome young men in the kingdom will be there," they cried. "We must look our best."

"Please may I come to the ball?" begged Cinderella.

"You go to the ball . . . don't be so ridiculous."

Her step-mother glared at Cinderella and said,

"You cannot go to the ball. You will have plenty of work to do once you have helped your sisters get ready."

Anyone but Cinderella would have refused to help, but she was so kind-hearted that she could not.

On the night of the ball the step-sisters had Cinderella running round in circles after them.

"Iron my dress . . . Brush my hair . . . Find my shoes."

At long last they were ready and, without a thank you or a wave goodbye, the step-sisters climbed into their carriage leaving Cinderella crying quietly all on her own next to the hearth.

"Oh, I wish I could have gone to the ball . . . I know I have nothing to wear, but I would have loved to have gone."

Suddenly, Cinderella heard a kind voice saying,

"I am your Fairy Godmother. Dry your eyes. You shall go to the ball. Just do as I ask."

Cinderella stared at the old lady who had appeared from nowhere.

"My very own Fairy Godmother. I will do as you ask," smiled Cinderella happily.

First she sent Cinderella to the garden for a pumpkin. She touched it with her magic wand and in an instant it became the most splendid coach you ever saw.

Then she asked her to bring the mousetrap from the kitchen. Inside were six white mice. The Fairy Godmother gave each a tap with her wand. Four little mice turned into magnificent white horses and the other two were changed into two fine footmen.

"Well now, Cinderella, you can go to the ball after all."

"But how can I go in these old rags?" cried Cinderella.

At once her Fairy Godmother waved her magic wand and transformed the rags into a beautiful gown, fit for a princess, and the daintiest glass slippers appeared on her feet.

"Now, off you go and enjoy yourself," said her Fairy Godmother. "But remember, you must not stay a second after midnight or all your fine clothes will turn back into rags."

"I promise I will not," said Cinderella as she set off for the ball.

When Cinderella arrived at the Palace a murmur ran around the crowd.

"Who is that beautiful girl?"

The Prince could not take his eyes off her and insisted on dancing with her for the whole evening.

Cinderella was so happy that she forgot all about the time until she heard the clock begin to strike twelve.

"Goodbye, Your Highness. I must go."

With these words, she fled from the ballroom.

In her haste Cinderella did not notice a glass slipper fall from her foot.

The Prince ran after her but she had vanished. Only the glass slipper remained.

"I will find her and make her my bride," vowed the Prince.

He sent out messengers with the glass slipper which they were to try on every girl

in the land. They finally came to Cinderella's house. The step-sisters tried it on but it would not fit.

"Why don't you try it on?" the messenger asked Cinderella.

"It won't fit," cried one step-sister. "Anyway, she wasn't at the ball."

The glass slipper fitted.

Her Fairy Godmother appeared and tapped Cinderella with her magic wand. Once more her clothes were beautiful and the messengers took her to the Palace. The Prince was overjoyed to see Cinderella.

Soon the couple were married. Everyone went to the wedding including her step-sisters whom Cinderella had completely forgiven for their previous unkindness.

The Ugly Duckling

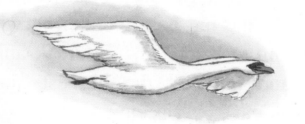

The Ugly Duckling

Once upon a time a duck sat patiently on her nest in the long grass by the river, waiting for her eggs to hatch. Suddenly the first shell cracked and out tumbled a little, yellow duckling. Then, one by one, out came the ducklings as each egg broke; that is except the biggest egg of all.

The mother duck gathered the ducklings to her and looked at the big egg, wondering why it was taking so long to hatch. Then a crack appeared in the shell and out fell the biggest and ugliest duckling you have ever seen.

"Come along, children," said the mother duck. "Come to the river and learn to swim."

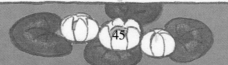

So off they went to the water. Soon all the ducklings were swimming happily after their mother, but the ugly duckling was right at the back because the others laughed at him for being so big and so ugly and so different, even though he swam as well as they did.

The mother duck then took her family along to the farmyard and said,

"Now, children, this is where we will live. Stay close to me, keep away from the big cat and mind you are polite to the big rooster."

All the creatures there greeted the ducklings as they arrived but they laughed when they saw the ugly duckling and he felt very lonely and unhappy.

The poor, ugly duckling was so unhappy because everyone teased' him that he ran away to the river but, even there, the creatures who saw him said,

"Goodness me, isn't he big! Isn't he ugly!"

The ugly duckling hid in the reeds and a tear dripped down his beak.

He decided to go right away and that night he set off across the fields and came to a little cottage. The old woman who lived there found him huddled on the doorstep and took him in.

Even there he was not welcome for the cat hissed at him because he could not catch mice and then hen pecked him because he could not lay eggs.

So, off he went on his travels again-across fields, over ditches and through woods-feeling more and more sad and unhappy. One day he looked up and saw some swans flying overhead.

"Oh, they are so beautiful. I wish I could be like them. I'm sure nobody laughs at them and teases them."

The poor, lonely, ugly duckling went on his way but by now summer was ending and the weather was becoming colder and food more difficult to find.

One day it was very cold and he was so tired he went to sleep while he was floating in a pond. When he awoke he could not move for the water had frozen around him while he slept.

Poor ugly duckling! He was all alone and frozen in the ice. Then he heard footsteps and saw a woodcutter coming. The duckling gave a feeble, little quack and the man went over to the pond.

"Well, what have we here? Stuck are you? Never mind, I'll soon have you free," he said and, with a few blows from his axe, he broke the ice and freed the poor, little bird. Tucking the ugly duckling under his arm he set off for home saying,' 'I think I'll take you home to thaw you out properly."

At his cottage he wrapped the ugly duckling up to keep him warm and told his children to look after him.

The two children were pleased to have a pet to care for and they kept the ugly duckling warm and fed him. When he had thawed out and was able to walk around again the children wanted to play with him but he was frightened and ran all around the room and knocked over the milk and eggs and the flour. The children's mother was cross when she saw all the mess and shouted,

"Outside with him! He can't stay inside here now he's better."

So, once more, the unwanted, ugly duckling ran away. He found his way to a small pond where he spent the rest of the winter, all alone and only just managing to find enough to eat.

At last the spring came, with soft breezes and warmer days, and the ugly duckling left his safe hiding place in the reeds around the pond. He spread his wings and found he could fly for, during the long, cold, dark days of winter, he had grown. He flew high above the countryside and, looking down, he saw, swimming in a lake, three of the swans he had watched when he was running away the previous year.

They looked up and called to him to join them. Hardly daring to believe that anyone wanted him he flew down. As he landed he saw his reflection in the water and cried out in joy,

"I'm a swan! I'm a swan!"

The Gingerbread Man

The Gingerbread Man

There was once an old woman who loved baking. One day, she was baking gingerbread and had enough mixture to make three big loaves with a little left over. Smiling to herself, she moulded the sticky mixture into the shape of a little man. She added currant eyes, nose and mouth and gave him four little currant buttons down his front.

"This will be a treat for my husband," she said.

When her husband came home the old woman opened the oven door and took out the loaves. Then she lifted out the gingerbread man.

"What a lovely surprise! I shall eat him after my supper," said the old man.

At these words, the gingerbread man suddenly came to life.

"Oh no, you WON'T!" he declared loudly, jumped to his feet, leapt down from the table and ran out of the door.

The old woman and the old man, astonished at this strange happening, gave chase at once but the gingerbread man was too fast for them.

"Run, run, as fast as you can!" he cried. "You can't catch me, I'm the gingerbread man!"

A dog saw the gingerbread man as he ran by.

"Mm! Very tasty," he thought and joined the chase but the gingerbread man only laughed.

On ran the gingerbread man with the old woman, the old man and the dog all chasing him.

He passed a boy kicking stones along the road and when the boy saw the gingerbread man he stopped and exclaimed,

"A gingerbread man! I would love to eat that."

So he began to chase him as well but the gingerbread man just laughed and said,

"Run, run, as fast as you can! You can't catch me, I'm the gingerbread man!"

The gingerbread man ran on and soon passed two road-menders. When they saw him, they dropped their shovels and ran after him.

"A gingerbread man! Just right for our tea."

The gingerbread man only laughed and said,

"Run, run, as fast as you can! You can't catch me, I'm the gingerbread man!"

The chase continued and soon they passed a horse, grazing in the field. The horse saw the gingerbread man and licked his lips.

"A gingerbread man would be a nice change from grass," he said, jumping over the fence, but the gingerbread man only laughed and said,

"Run, run, as fast as you can! You can't catch me, I'm the gingerbread man!"

The horse could gallop fast but not fast enough. The gingerbread man ran like the wind laughing all the time as he went along.

"Run, run!" he called out gleefully. "Run, run, as fast as you can! You can't catch me, I'm the gingerbread man!"

And those that ran after him puffed and panted more and more.

The gingerbread man began to run through the fields and still he laughed. The old woman, the old man, the dog, the boy, the road-menders and the horse still chased him but they were falling further back and could not carry on much longer.

Then, suddenly, the gingerbread man stopped. He had come to a deep and fast-flowing river too wide to jump across. There was no bridge and he could not swim. The old woman, the old man, the dog, the boy, the road-menders and the horse were still coming after him, so he could not go back.

"What shall I do?" he said to himself. "They must not catch the gingerbread man!"

At that moment, the gingerbread man heard a silky-smooth voice in his ear, saying,

"I can help you get across the river."

The gingerbread man turned and saw a fox standing beside him, smiling.

"Jump on to my back and I'll carry you across, if you like," said the fox.

"Mind you don't get me wet!" he said and then he turned to laugh at the old woman, the old man, the dog, the boy, the road-menders and the horse, who were all running towards the river-bank.

"Run, run, as fast as you can! You can't catch me, I'm the gingerbread man!"

The fox waded to the middle of the river.

"The water's getting deeper now," he told the gingerbread man. "You had better climb higher."

The gingerbread man did as he was told.

"The water is getting deeper still," warned the fox. "Climb on to my head or you will get wet!"

He climbed up and, looking back at the river-bank, where the old woman, the old man, the dog, the boy, the road-menders and the horse were standing, he called out,

"Run, run, as fast as you can! You can't catch me, I'm the gingerbread man!"

They all watched as the fox spoke again,

"It's still too deep! Climb on to the tip of my nose if you want to stay out of the water!"

He climbed up on to the tip of the fox's nose and, as they watched, the fox tossed him up in the air and caught him with a snap of his jaws. The gingerbread man was gone in one gulp.

"Well," said the old woman. "That's the last time I make one of those!"

The fox smiled. He knew that you had to be smart to catch a gingerbread man.

The Little Mermaid

The Little Mermaid

Once upon a time there was a little mermaid, the youngest, and most beautiful, daughter of the Mer King. She lived with her father, grandmother and five sisters in a palace of shells, deep, deep in the ocean. The mermaids longed to see the world above that their grandmother had described but each had to wait until her fifteenth birthday.

At last her birthday came and the little mermaid rose to the surface and gazed about in wonder.

A large galleon was nearby and she could hear music. A Prince was celebrating his birthday and she thought he was the most handsome being she had ever seen.

Suddenly a storm blew up. The waves grew higher until at last they overwhelmed the proud ship. She was horrified to see the Prince sinking, apparently lifeless. She swam quickly to him and pulled him to the surface.

When the storm passed she took him to land and laid him on a beach and then shyly hid to see what would happen.

Some girls found the Prince and he was taken to their castle and the little mermaid swam back to her father's palace thinking sadly that the Prince would never know it was she who had saved him and that she would never see him again.

One of her sisters knew the palace where the Prince lived so the little mermaid spent hours watching him for she had fallen deeply in love.

Her grandmother explained that merpeople live for three hundred years but when they die they become sea-foam, as they have no souls. She said that humans, although they only live for a short time, have souls and so, when they die, go to a wonderful place far away.

"Is there any way I can get a soul?" asked the little mermaid.

"Only if a human falls in love with you and that is unlikely for humans like legs not tails"

In desperation she sought help from the Sea Witch. It was a terrifying, dangerous journey but the thought of the Prince gave her courage.

"So you want legs? Foolish child! Losing your tail is painful and walking on feet will be like walking on knives. If he loves another you will become sea-foam."

"Please, I still want to try."

"I must have your voice in payment for this potion," growled the Witch and, so in love was the little mermaid, she agreed.

She swam to the Prince's palace before she drank the potion. She felt a sharp pain, fell into a deep sleep and awoke with human legs.

The Prince asked who the lovely stranger was but she could only smile. He grew fond of the girl with the sweet smile who danced so elegantly (even though it was as if she danced on knives) but he did not ask her to marry him and one day he told her he was to marry a foreign princess.

"I am sure I can love only the girl I glimpsed when she saved me from drowning. You look a little like her and if I must marry someone else I would rather marry you."

Her eyes filled with tears for she could not speak to tell him the truth.

The little mermaid travelled with the Prince to his wedding and he was glad when he found his bride was one of the girls who had found him on the beach because he thought she was his rescuer and fell in love with her.

At the feast on the Prince's ship after the wedding the little mermaid thought her heart would break.

She wept, for at dawn she would die and become sea-foam. As she stood there her sisters came, pale and with all their long hair gone.

"We gave our hair to the Sea Witch as payment for a magic knife. If you kill the Prince with it before dawn you will be a mermaid again," they cried.

They gave her the knife and she went to where the Prince was asleep but, even to save herself, she could not kill him and, with one last loving look, she threw herself into the sea and became sea-foam.

As the sun rose higher she found herself high in the sky.

"Where am I?" she asked and the reply came from sweet voices in the glowing lights around her.

"You are with the Children of the Air. We earn our souls by helping those who suffer and you can earn a soul too."

Below the Prince and his bride sailed on not knowing the little mermaid was smiling down at them.

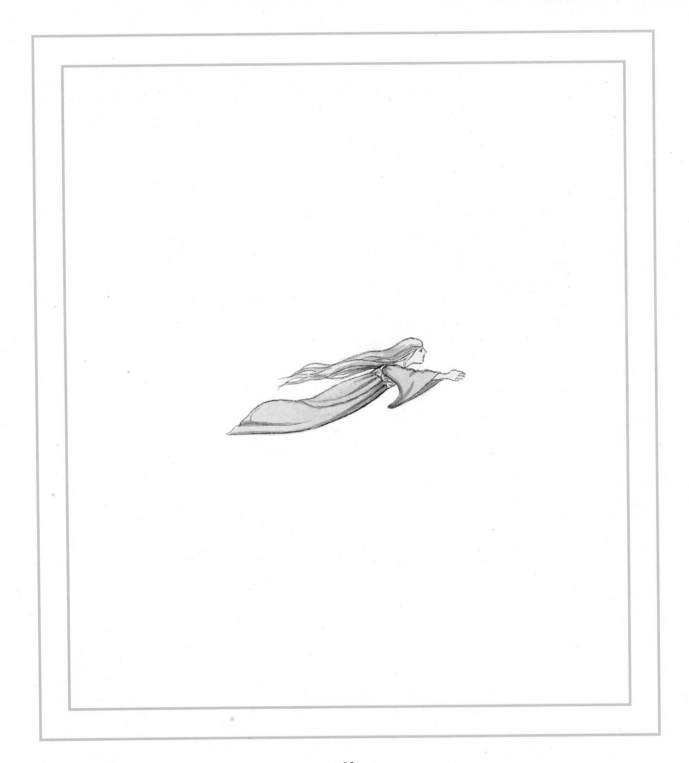

The Elves and the Shoemaker

The Elves and the Shoemaker

Once upon a time there was a shoemaker who, through no fault of his own, had become so poor that he had only enough leather left for one more pair of shoes.

"I must make these shoes the best ones I have ever made," he said to himself, "for they could be the last I ever make."

So he carefully cut the leather out and left the pieces ready to sew the next day when it was daylight. Then he blew out the candle and crept into bed.

Next morning he went to begin work and could hardly believe what he saw.

There on his workbench was the pair of shoes already made. He picked them up and looked at them.

"Well," he said, "not a stitch out of place. These shoes have been made by a master craftsman."

He put them in his window and that very day a customer came in to buy them.

"These shoes are the finest I have ever seen," cried the man and paid more than the usual price.

With the money, the shoemaker was able to buy enough leather to make two pairs of shoes and that night he cut it out and left it ready to sew the next day.

Once again, he found the shoes had already been sewn. Two beautiful pairs of shoes sat on the bench. Again he sold these for more than the usual price and had enough money to buy the leather for four pairs of shoes and these, too, he sold for a lot of money.

This went on for many days and soon the old shoemaker was making a comfortable living and no longer feared the future.

One day, just before Christmas, he said to his wife,

"Let's stay up late tonight, hide in the workshop and see if we can find out who has been helping us."

That night the two of them hid behind a cupboard in a corner of the workshop and waited to see if anything would happen. As the church clock struck midnight two tiny, barefoot elves in ragged clothes ran into the room. They climbed on the workbench and began stitching and sewing, as quickly as could be, all the leather that the shoemaker had left there.

The shoemaker and his wife watched in disbelief as the two tiny elves used up all the leather, neatly put the shoes they had made in pairs on the bench and then disappeared as quickly as they had come.

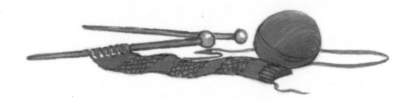

The old couple went to bed and next day the shoemaker's wife said to her husband,

"Those two elves have made us rich and I think we should show them how grateful we are."

He agreed and asked what they should do.

"Well," said his wife, "their clothes were ragged and they had no shoes on their feet so I think they must be very cold this winter. I will make them each little shirts, trousers and jackets and knit them long woollen socks and you can make them each a pair of shoes."

So that is what they did.

The shoemaker and his wife worked hard making the two suits and the two pairs of shoes for the elves. She knitted long, warm woollen stockings when she had finished the suits and then said to her husband,

"I think I have enough material to make hats for them too. Go to the chicken run and get me two long feathers to put in the hatbands. That will look very smart."

On Christmas Eve everything was finished and the shoemaker's wife wrapped all the clothes up into two little parcels and the shoemaker put them on the workbench instead of the pile of pieces of leather.

Again they hid and waited to see what would happen.

As midnight struck the two tiny elves appeared and scampered to the workbench and stopped in surprise at seeing the two parcels.

Chuckling, they opened them and burst into delighted laughter. They threw off their tattered clothes and dressed in the fine, new ones. Then they danced across the bench singing,

"Now we are so fine to see,

We will no longer work, not we."

Dancing and singing they ran across the floor and out of the door and were never seen again.

Nevertheless, the shoemaker continued to prosper and he and his wife lived happily ever after.

The House That Jack Built

The House That Jack Built

This is the house that Jack built.

This is the malt,
That lay in the house that Jack built.

This is the rat,
That ate the malt,
That lay in the house that Jack built.

This is the cat,
That killed the rat,
That ate the malt,
That lay in the house that Jack built.

This is the dog,
That worried the cat,
That killed the rat,
That ate the malt,
That lay in the house that Jack built.

This is the cow with the crumpled horn,
That tossed the dog,
That worried the cat,
That killed the rat,
That ate the malt,
That lay in the house that Jack built.

This is the maiden all forlorn,
That milked the cow with the crumpled horn,
That tossed the dog,
That worried the cat,
That killed the rat,
That ate the malt,
That lay in the house that Jack built.

This is the man all tattered and torn,
That kissed the maiden all forlorn,
That milked the cow with the crumpled horn,
That tossed the dog,
That worried the cat,
That killed the rat,
That ate the malt,
That lay in the house that Jack built.

This is the priest all shaven and shorn,
That married the man all tattered and torn,
That kissed the maiden all forlorn,
That milked the cow with the crumpled horn,

That tossed the dog,
That worried the cat,
That killed the rat,
That ate the malt,
That lay in the house that Jack built.

This is the cock that crowed in the morn,
That woke the priest all shaven and shorn,
That married the man all tattered and torn,
That kissed the maiden all forlorn,
That milked the cow with the crumpled horn,

That tossed the dog,
That worried the cat,
That killed the rat,
That ate the malt,
That lay in the house that Jack built.

This is the farmer that sowed the corn,
That fed the cock that crowed in the morn,
That woke the priest all shaven and shorn,
That married the man all tattered and torn,
That kissed the maiden all forlorn,
That milked the cow with the crumpled horn,

That tossed the dog,
That worried the cat,
That killed the rat,
That ate the malt,
That lay in the house that Jack built.

That was the house that Jack built.

Sleeping Beauty

Sleeping Beauty

Once upon a time, in a far-off land, there lived a King and Queen who longed for a baby. Many years passed before their wish came true and a baby girl was born. The King and Queen were very happy and so they gave a huge banquet. They invited all their friends and there was much rejoicing in the palace.

The fairies of the kingdom had also been invited and after the banquet all the good fairies went to the little Princess's nursery. One by one they wished that she would grow up to be beautiful, clever and good.

The good fairies were busy making their wishes when, suddenly, the door opened and in walked the bad fairy.

"Why have I been left out?" she cried. "Why wasn't I invited to the banquet?"

Somehow, the King and Queen had forgotten to invite her.

Leaning over the baby's crib the bad fairy said,

"When you reach your fifteenth birthday you will be pricked by the spindle of a spinning wheel and will die."

With that she disappeared in a puff of smoke.

The last fairy had not yet bestowed her gift so she wished that the Princess would not die but only sleep for one hundred years.

The King ordered that all the spinning wheels in the country were to be destroyed.

The years passed and the little Princess grew into a beautiful, young girl. The bad fairy's curse was forgotten and everyone in the palace was happy.

On her fifteenth birthday the Princess was exploring the palace and opened a door at the top of an old staircase. Inside the room she saw an old woman turning a strange wheel.

"What are you doing?" asked the Princess who, of course, had never seen a spinning wheel before.

"I am spinning," said the old woman. "Would you like to try?"

As soon as the Princess picked up the spindle she pricked her finger and fell to the floor in a deep sleep.

When the King and Queen found her they laid her down on her bed. The good fairies came and said that the Princess would only wake up when a Prince kissed her and, so that she would not be on her own during her long sleep, they waved their wands and everyone and everything in the palace fell asleep.

King, Queen, soldiers, courtiers and servants, horses, dogs, mice and rats, all slept and while they slept a magic forest grew round the palace to protect it.

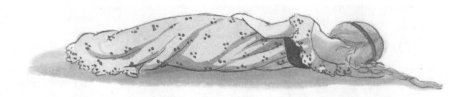

Years passed and, as legends about the beautiful, sleeping Princess grew, many young men tried to reach the palace but all failed to pierce the magic forest.

Exactly one hundred years later, to the day, a young Prince was hunting near the palace and asked a woodcutter about it.

"My old grandfather told me a curse was put on the Princess and that she is inside, fast asleep, with all the people in the palace, and that she can only be awoken by the kiss of a Prince. No-one has ever managed to get through that forest, though," added the woodcutter.

The Prince listened in growing excitement to the story and decided he would be the Prince who would awaken the sleeping Princess. He thanked the woodcutter and made his way towards the forest round the palace.

As he approached he took out his sword but was astounded to find the branches parting

before him and that he had no need to struggle.

As the palace gates came into view he could see the sleeping guards. He pushed the gates open and went in. The whole palace was asleep, even the dogs in the kennels.

The brave, young Prince made his way through dusty rooms searching for the sleeping Princess.

At last he found her lying on her bed. She looked so beautiful and peaceful as she lay there.

He knelt down and very gently kissed her on the lips. Her eyes opened and she awoke.

Soon all the palace was rousing from its long sleep. Courtiers, soldiers, cooks and stablemen - all awoke and stretched and wondered what was happening. The King and Queen hurried to see their daughter and found her wide awake at last.

The Prince and the Princess fell in love and the King and Queen happily agreed to the marriage and they all lived happily ever after.

The Hare and The Tortoise

The Hare and The Tortoise

It was a lovely, sunny day, but the animals in the forest were paying no attention to the weather. They were arguing about which of them could run the fastest. Hare, as usual, was boasting.

"I am the fastest by far! I will race any of you. The prize will be this gold button. Squirrel, how about you?"

"No fear, Hare, not I," giggled Squirrel.

"Fox, do you want to race me?"

Fox shook his head silently.

"Is nobody brave enough to try to beat me in a race? Badger? Hedgehog? Weasel? . . . Nobody?"

There was silence for a minute or two and then a tiny voice said,

"I'll have a try, if you like."

Hare turned round and saw Tortoise plodding slowly across the field at the edge of the forest.

Hare giggled quietly to himself and tried to keep his face straight as he spoke to Tortoise.

"Ah, Tortoise! So you are here - at last!"

"I saw no reason to hurry," said Tortoise. "It's such a lovely day, after all."

"It seems that you are my only challenger. Are you willing to race me to the stone bridge on the other side of the wood for this fine prize?"

"It certainly is a fine prize and a race to the bridge sounds fair enough. Yes, I am willing to race you," said Tortoise slowly and carefully.

"Old Slowcoach!" laughed Hare. "You *must* be joking! You have no chance of beating me!"

The other animals joined in the laughter but Tortoise shook his head slowly.

"Indeed I am not joking!" he said. "Now, who is going to start us off?"

Hare was still laughing as the two animals lined up and waited for Owl's starting signal.

"Tu-whit-tu-whoo!"

The 'tu-whoo' had hardly left Owl's beak when Hare was off like the wind, speeding through the trees. Tortoise was still plodding into the edge of the woods when Hare was out of sight.

"Come on, Tortoise!" cheered the other animals laughing. "Can't you go faster than that?"

"I don't know why you bother," said Badger.

"Hare will win by miles," said Hedgehog.

Tortoise did not show that he was hurt by these unkind remarks. Instead, he just kept plodding on, all the time saying to himself,

"Slow and steady wins the race: slow and steady ..."

Hare charged relentlessly on through the woods. He looked back but there was no sign of Tortoise so he lolloped on more gently for a few more minutes and then stopped again. He was now at the far edge of the wood and, in front of him, he could see the old, stone bridge - the finishing post of the race.

Hare, being a bit of a show-off, did not like the idea of finishing with no-one there to cheer him so he sat down under a tree to wait until the other animals caught up. Then he would make a triumphant dash for the bridge. It was a hot day, however, and Hare had to close his eyes against the glare of the sun. In the twinkling of an eye he had dozed off to sleep.

It was late afternoon when Hare woke up and the sun was no longer fierce and hot. As he got up he caught the sound of the other animals in a state of excitement - twittering, squeaking and hooting.

"Goody!" he thought. "They're here to see me win. Poor old Tortoise. He'll be miles behind."

Hare had a little stretch and got ready to run again. He did not know, however, that, all the time he had been sleeping, Tortoise had been trudging slowly but steadily on through the woods. In fact Hare had been asleep long enough for Tortoise to catch up with him and pass him and he did not realize that the animals were cheering Tortoise and not him!

Tortoise was now only a couple of steps away from the old, stone bridge. All of a sudden, Hare caught sight of Tortoise and, with horror, realized what had happened.

He could not believe how foolish he had been. It did not matter now how hard he ran for it was too late to catch up with Tortoise and all the other animals were there to see Tortoise win.

Tortoise plodded the last step to the bridge and stood there glowing with pride. It was one of the happiest days of his life. He had beaten Hare and the other animals cheered him.

"Good old Tortoise! You've won! Well done!"

Poor Hare! How silly he felt to think of everybody watching him sleeping as Tortoise passed him! He wished he had never boasted.

"Here you are. Here's the gold button prize," he muttered, ears drooping. "And - well done!"

"You can keep the button, Hare," said Tortoise kindly. "I've had a lot of fun today. Just remember; slow and steady wins the race, slow and steady . . ."

Rapunzel

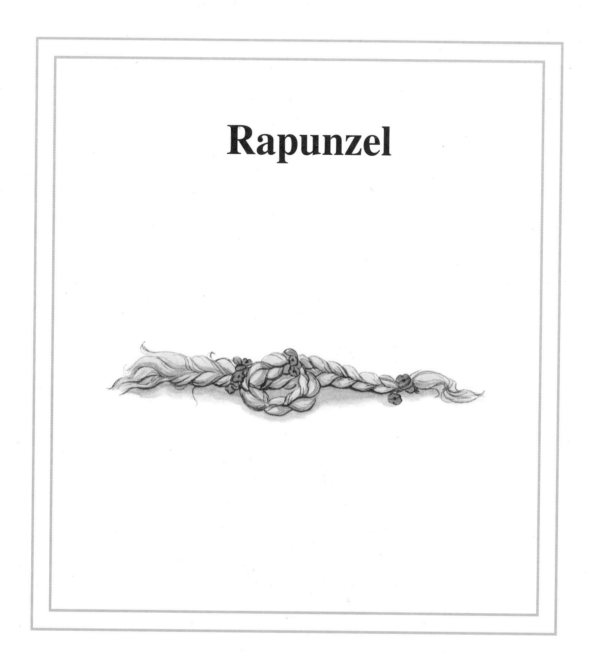

Rapunzel

Once upon a time a husband and wife lived happily in a house whose upstairs window overlooked a beautiful garden. In this garden everything grew in profusion. The trees were laden with fruit and the flowers were brightly coloured. One day as the wife hung out her washing she noticed how well the rapunzel herb had grown. From then on each day she would sit at the window longing for a taste.

However, as a horrid witch lived next door, whom everyone feared, she knew that she would not be able to have any and began to pine away and grow weak and ill.

Her husband, fearing for her life, decided to take matters into his own hands. He climbed over the high wall and filled his basket with the rapunzel herb. The witch caught him in the act.

"How dare you come into my garden and steal my herbs!" she cried angrily.

The terrified man told the witch about his wife's craving and how he hoped the rapunzel would cure her and the witch eventually allowed him to take the herb on the condition that they would give her their first-born child. The man nodded his head in agreement and rushed back to his wife.

The herb did make her well and not long afterwards she had a baby girl. The witch came and took the baby away and named her Rapunzel after the herb.

The years passed and the couple could only watch their child from the upstairs window as she played happily in the witch's garden.

She was such a pretty little girl with long, golden hair.

When Rapunzel was twelve years old the witch decided to lock her in a high tower so she could not run away. When Rapunzel was in the topmost room the witch put a spell on the staircase and door so Rapunzel could not find them.

Rapunzel's hair was in a long plait. Each day, when the witch visited her, she would call out,

"Rapunzel, Rapunzel,

Let down your long hair!"

Rapunzel would let her long plait fall down the tower and the witch would climb up it.

One day a passing Prince heard the witch calling out and could not believe it when he saw the plait come down and the witch climb up it. As he was full of curiosity he waited until the witch had left and then he called out,

"Rapunzel, Rapunzel,

Let down your long hair!"

When the plait came down the Prince climbed up it and was amazed to see the beautiful girl. Gently, he began talking to her and soon Rapunzel and he became friends. The Prince visited her often after that as he loved to hear her sing.

One day, however, Rapunzel asked the witch, "Why is it that the Prince climbs up my hair so much faster than you do?"

The witch was very angry at being deceived and the next day, when she visited Rapunzel, she cut off her hair and led her deep into the forest where she abandoned her.

The witch returned to the tower and, when the Prince called out, she tied the plait to the window and let it down. What a shock the Prince got when he saw the witch.

"You will never see Rapunzel again," she screeched as she pulled his hands from the hair.

The Prince fell headlong into a clump of thorny bushes. They broke his fall but their thorns scratched his eyes so that he could not see. His horse had fled at the sound of the witch's voice and the Prince stumbled around the forest for many days, surviving on berries and water from streams.

Over the weeks the Prince had gradually become accustomed to the sounds of the forest as he wandered blind and lonely through the countryside but, one day, he heard a new sound he thought he recognised. Rapunzel was singing. He stumbled towards the sound calling her name.

Suddenly Rapunzel saw him and ran into his arms. As she kissed him his eyes were healed and he could see her.

The Prince took Rapunzel to meet his father and when he heard the story he banished the witch from the kingdom.

Rapunzel was reunited with her parents and later she and the Prince were married.

The Emperor's New Clothes

The Emperor's New Clothes

A long time ago in a country far away, there ruled an emperor. He was very vain and loved to parade in front of his people at the head of grand processions, magnificently dressed in regal robes.

All the tailors in the country vied with each other to be allowed to make clothes for him.

One day two men arrived at the palace, told the guards they were tailors and asked to see the emperor. He agreed to see them and was amazed at what they said.

"Your Majesty, we wish to make you superb robes from a special cloth. We will weave this cloth on our own looms and it has magic powers.

"A wise person will be able to see the magnificent cloth but a fool will see nothing. We have chosen you to be the first to wear this cloth for you are the most elegant man in the land."

The emperor was delighted. He gave the men a bag of gold and told them to start work at once. The two rascals set up their looms in a room in the palace. They gave orders for the finest gold and silver threads to be be brought but they did not use this thread. They packed it away in sacks to sell for a good price in the market and just pretended to work on the empty looms. As they left the palace that evening, they told the guards that the cloth was half-finished.

The next day they returned and pretended to be working on the empty looms once more.

The emperor had promised them that he would not look at the cloth before it was finished but, unable to contain his curiosity, he sent his man-servant to visit them at their work. He knew that the magic cloth was invisible to fools but was sure he would be wise enough to see it. However, when he went in he could only see the men working at what appeared to be empty looms.

"I cannot see the magic cloth, but how can I admit that to the emperor? I will lose my job," he thought and decided he would have to pretend.

"What do you think of our cloth?" they asked.

"Beautiful!" he replied. "How ever can I describe such amazing cloth to the emperor?"

"Describe it this way," the rascal grinned and gave him a long description of exotic cloth.

The emperor was even more excited after his manservant told him about the cloth and could hardly wait for it to be finished. Finally, the tailors came to say that they had completed the weaving and wanted him to see the cloth before they made it into robes so he went to the workroom and stared at the empty looms in dismay.

"I cannot see the magic cloth but if my people find out that I am a fool they will no longer have me as emperor so I will have to pretend," he thought to himself and said aloud to the tailors,

"This is the most beautiful cloth ever seen."

He ordered them to make the cloth into robes for him to wear in a grand, royal procession and the two rascals grinned to themselves while they pretended to work day and night on the robes.

On the morning of the great procession, the tailors went to the emperor and held up their hands as if they were holding up clothes for inspection.

"Our great work is complete, Your Majesty!" they announced. "We hope you are satisfied!"

The courtiers could see nothing at all but they pretended they could and agreed that the clothes were the most beautiful there had ever been.

"You are the most skilful of tailors," said the delighted emperor. "I shall reward you handsomely," he added as he went to his chambers where the tailors pretended to dress him in his new clothes.

Trying not to shiver with the cold, he stared into his mirror but, try as he could, he could see no clothes, just his own plump, pink body.

The rascally tailors were enjoying themselves.
"Isn't the robe perfection itself?" they said.

"It is quite the finest outfit I have ever worn," said the emperor but, secretly, he wished he were clever enough to see the clothes.

Soon the great procession set off. Everybody had come to see the new magic robes and, as the emperor went by, everyone thought the same thing.

"If I cannot see the clothes, I must be a fool!"

So, just as the emperor, his manservant and all the courtiers had done, they decided to pretend, for none of them wanted to be thought foolish.

"Look at the colours! Look at the style!"

The emperor's chest swelled with pride as he heard all the praise. It was so nice to be admired.

The procession passed by a young boy who had not been told about the magic robes. He took one look at the emperor and burst out laughing.

"The emperor has no clothes on!" he shouted and, all around, the people began to whisper,

"The boy is right! The emperor *is* naked!"

The boy had given people the courage to tell the truth and the emperor had heard the boy too. He blushed with embarrassment and realised that he was indeed naked and that he *was* a fool.

Somewhere far away, the two wily tailors were laughing at the foolish emperor and discussing how to spend the fortune they had made.

Meanwhile, the emperor returned as quickly as possible to the palace, cold and ashamed but much wiser. Never again would he let his vanity stop him from using his common sense.

Puss in Boots

Puss in Boots

Once upon a time there was a poor miller who had three sons who, when he died, left only his mill, his donkey and his cat. The eldest son took the mill, the second the donkey and the youngest was left with nothing but the cat.

"My brothers have done well," said the youngest son. "They can make a living with the mill and the donkey together but how can I manage?"

"Don't be sad, master," said the cat. "Just give me a sack and a pair of boots and you will soon see that you have the best bargain."

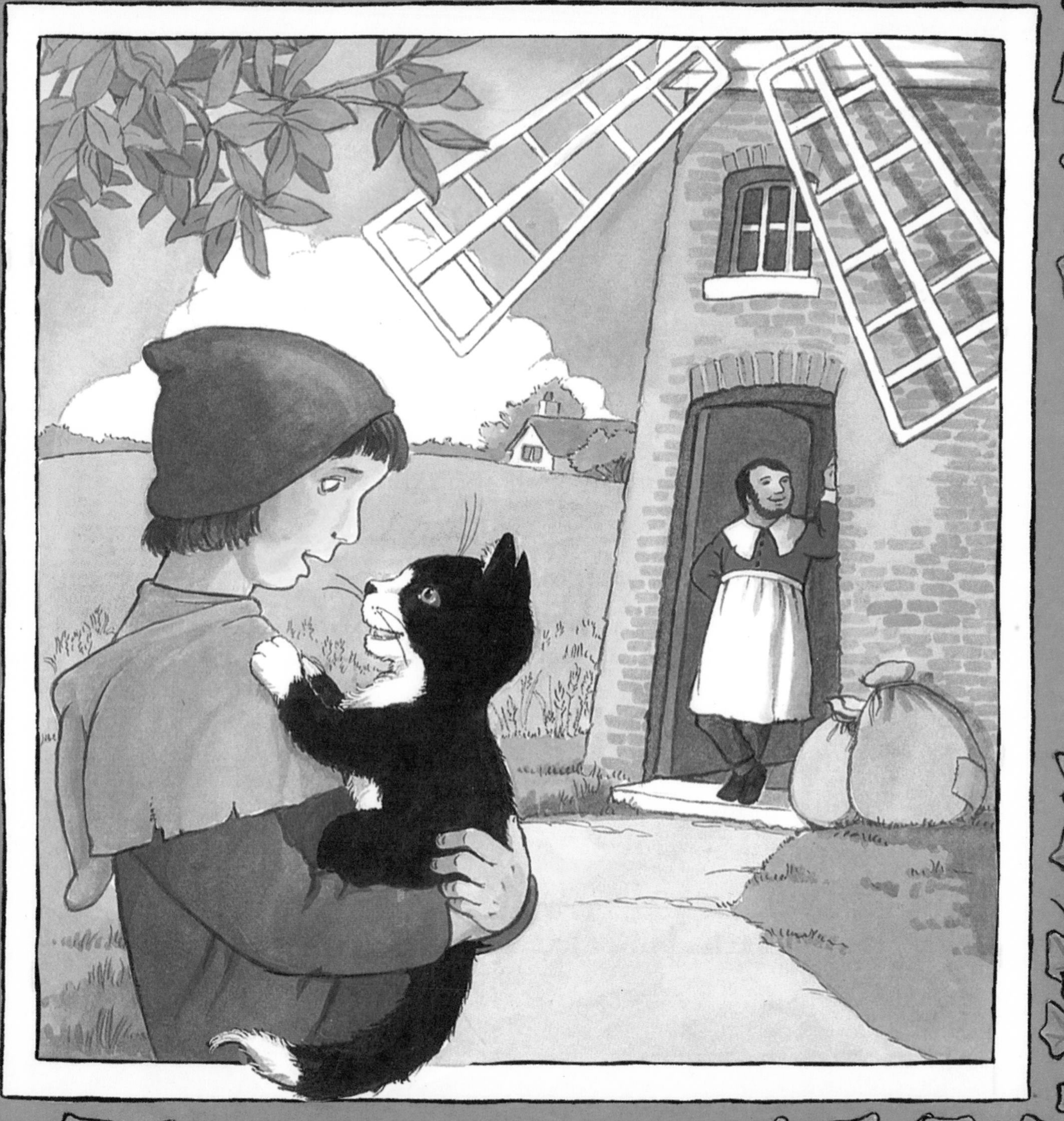

The miller's son was astonished to hear the cat talk.

"A talking cat might just be clever enough to do anything:' he thought, so he bought a pair of leather boots for the cat and said, "Well now, Puss in Boots, what are you going to do?"

"Wait and see!" said the cat and, swinging a sack over his shoulder, he set out into the woods.

He hid by a rabbit warren and soon tricked a silly young rabbit into his sack. Then off he went to the King's palace and demanded to see the King.

"Your Majesty," he said, "I have brought a gift from my master, the Marquis of Carabas." This was the title he had invented for the miller's son.

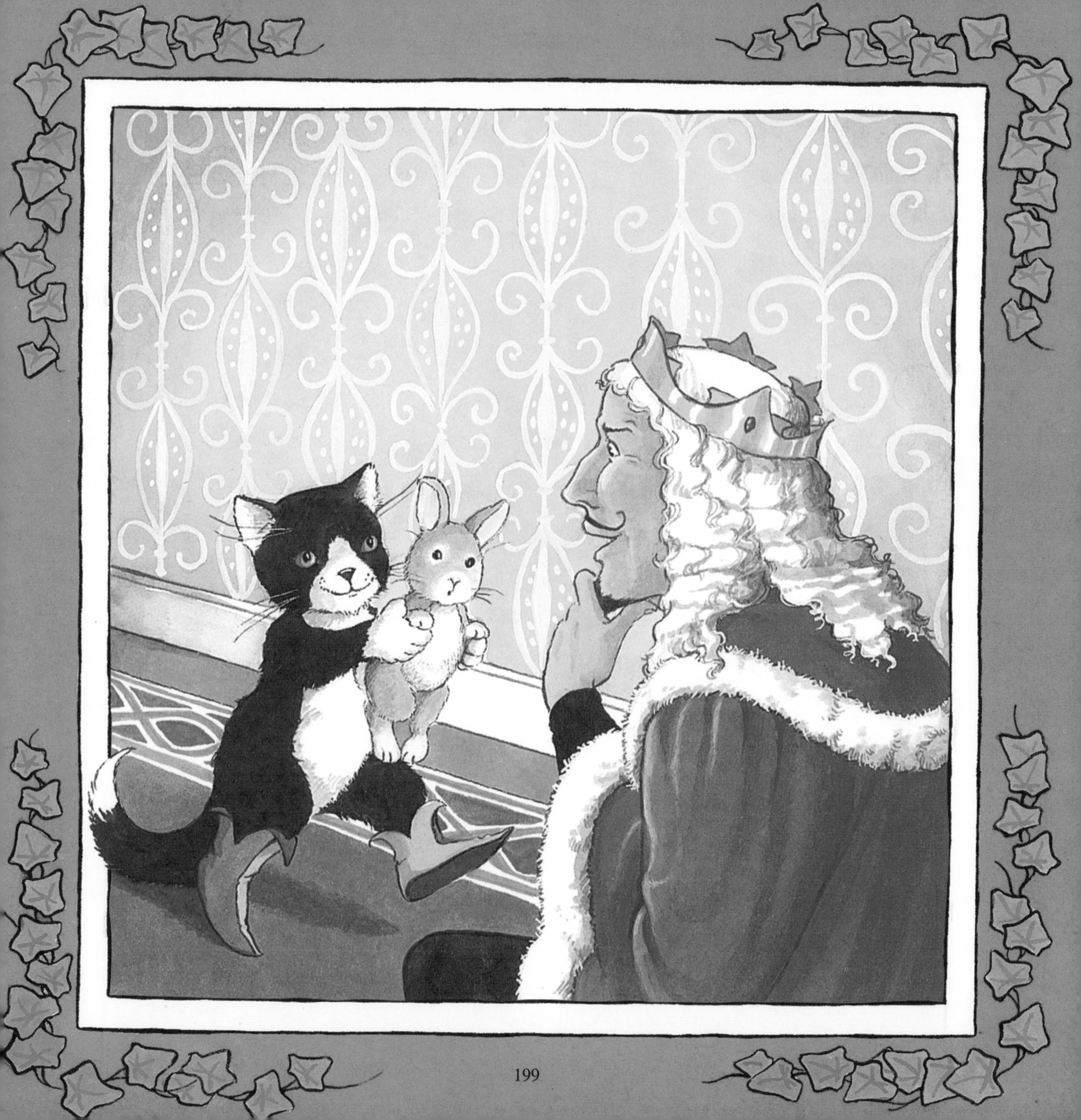

As the King was pleased with the rabbit, Puss brought him more gifts, each time saying they were from his master.

One day the cat heard that the King and his beautiful daughter were to drive by the river so he went to his master and said,

"Do just as I say and you will be rich. Go and bathe in the river."

He did as he was bid and the cat hid his clothes. As the royal coach came by the cat shouted,

"Help! My master, the Marquis of Carabas is drowning."

The King, recognising Puss, ordered his guards to save the young man.

"Thank you, Your Majesty," said Puss, "but what can my master do? His clothes have been stolen."

The King immediately sent for a suit of clothes and then invited the miller's son to ride with him. He looked so handsome in his new clothes that the beautiful Princess fell in love with him.

Meanwhile the cat hurried ahead, first to a field where some men were working and then to where a shepherd was with his sheep. He shouted to them all,

"The King is coming. Tell him the fields and the sheep belong to the Marquis of Carabas or you'll be in trouble."

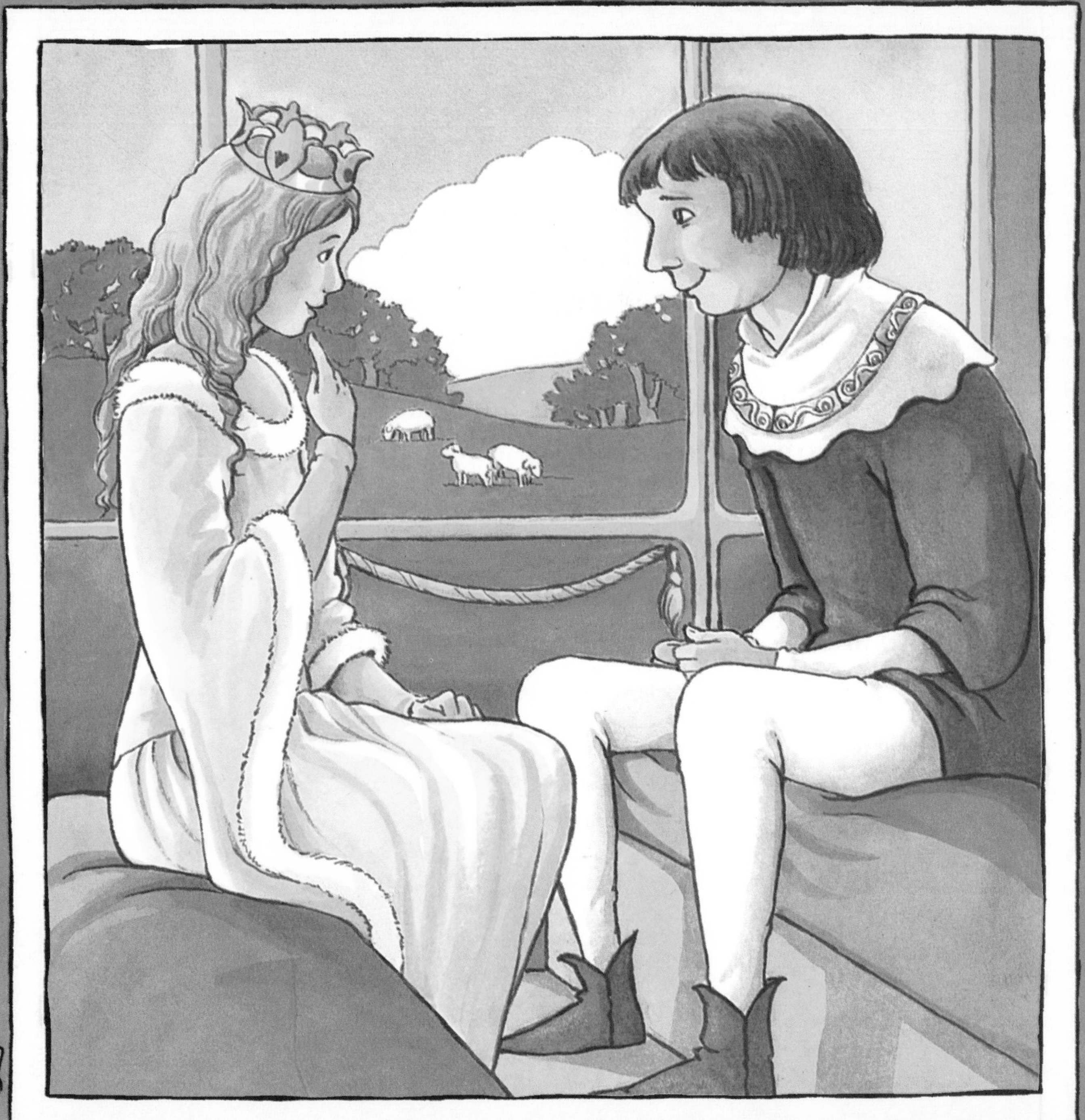

He looked so fierce that they did as he said.

Now the fields really belonged to an ogre who lived in a nearby castle. Puss knew of this ogre and called at the castle door.

"Sir," said Puss to the ogre, "I have been told you are able to turn yourself into an elephant or a lion."

"Indeed I can," said the ogre proudly and the next moment there stood a great lion which roared mightily.

Puss was so frightened that he jumped straight up to the top of a tall cupboard.

When the ogre changed himself back Puss jumped down.

"Well," said the cunning cat, "that was very fine but I have also heard it said that you can change yourself into something very small and I am sure that is impossible."

"Impossible?" growled the ogre, deeply insulted. "Nothing is impossible for me!"

In the twinkling of an eye there appeared a tiny fieldmouse scampering across the floor. With one leap the clever cat caught the mouse and gobbled him up and that was the end of the fierce ogre.

Meanwhile, the King, with his daughter and the miller's son, had seen the castle and decided to call on its owner.

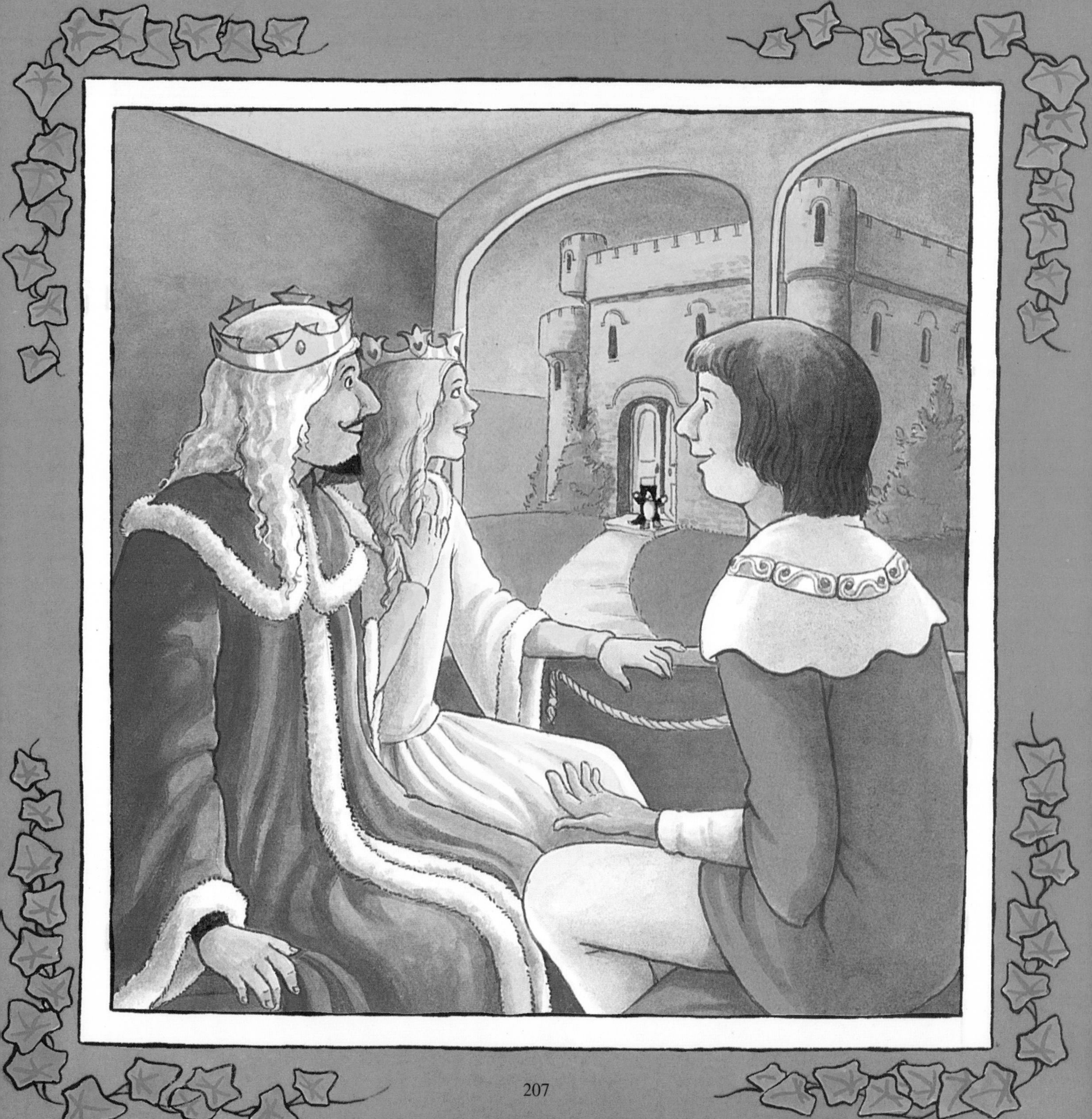

The coach rolled up to the castle door and there was Puss in Boots.

"Welcome to the castle of my master, the Marquis of Carabas!" he called, winking at the miller's son.

The King was delighted to see his new young friend lived in such a splendid castle and was pleased to be invited to the feast that had been prepared.

After the feast, the King declared that, since the Marquis and the Princess were obviously in love, they ought to get married. So they did and lived happily ever after.

As for Puss in Boots he lived off the fat of the land with his master until the end of his days!

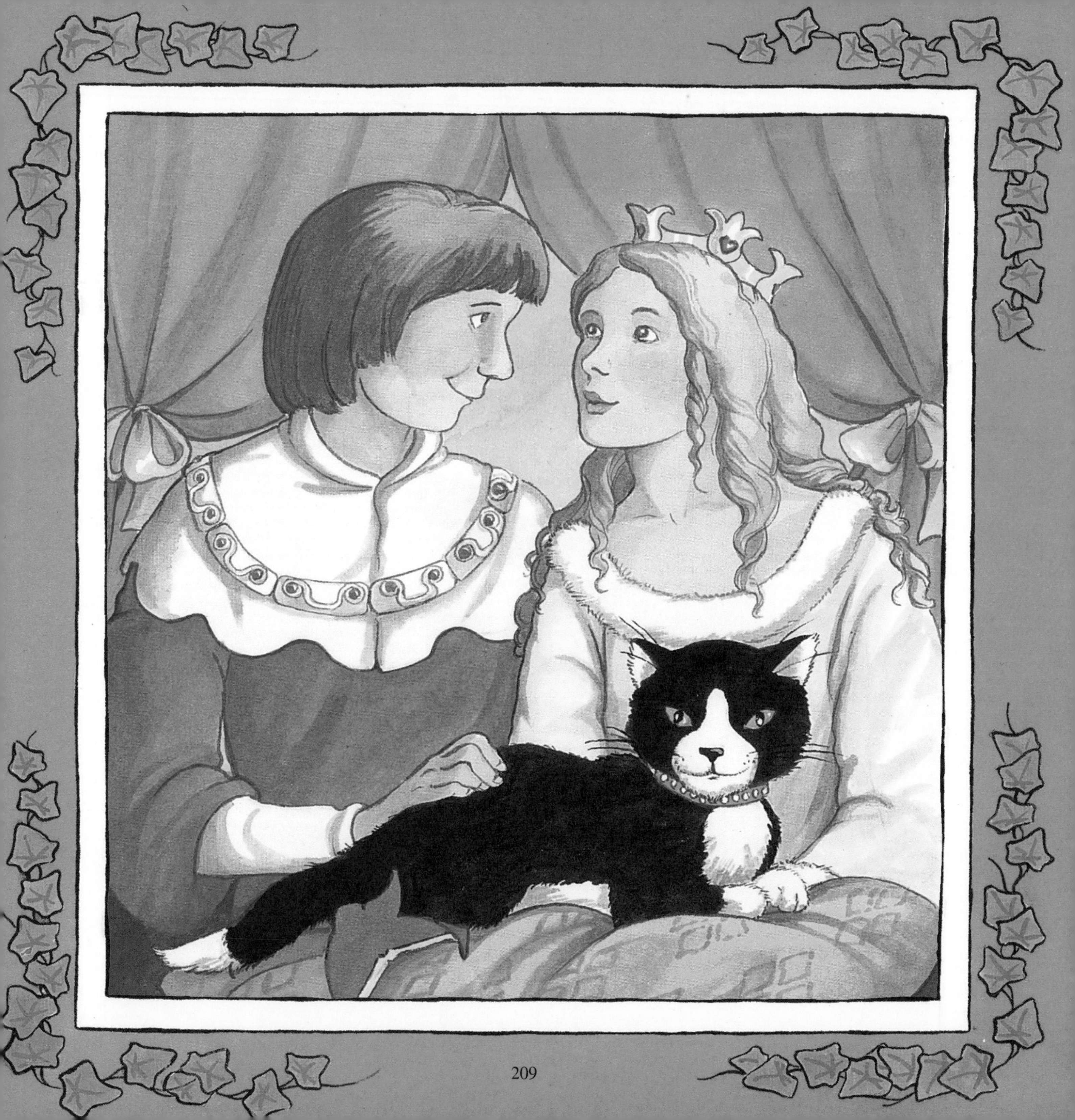

The Snow Queen

The Snow Queen

Once there was a wicked sorcerer who had made a magic mirror. In it everything, no matter how beautiful or good, looked ugly. The sorcerer showed it to the nasty little imps, his pupils, and they took the mirror everywhere. They even wanted to see how heaven would look in it.

As they flew, the mirror shook and shook until it slipped from their hands, breaking into a million pieces, some as small as a speck of dust. If a tiny grain were to get into a child's eye, everything that child saw would seem bad and if a piece reached a child's heart, that heart turned to ice!

Kay and Gerda lived opposite one another. They were very poor but each had a garden, with a rambler rose, where they often played.

One day Kay suddenly cried out,

"Oh, I've got something in my eye! Oh, my heart! Now it is in my heart!"

It was a splinter of the magic mirror and now poor Kay was quite changed. He saw everything twisted, his heart was frozen and he played alone.

While he was playing with his toboggan a white sledge appeared, drawn by a white horse. In it was a figure in white furs who told him to tie his toboggan to the sledge. He was scared but did so and the sledge sped off. When it stopped a beautiful lady stepped out - the Snow Queen. She kissed him lightly on the forehead, a kiss as cold as ice. Then she kissed him again.

Kay forgot the cold, Gerda and everyone else and was no longer afraid. The Snow Queen took him into her sledge and up they went in the air.

Oh, how bitterly little Gerda cried for Kay! Then spring came and the rose budded again.

"Kay is dead," Gerda told the swallows.

"We do not believe it," they twittered and, in the end, even Gerda could not think it was true.

"I will give you my new shoes if you will bring me to Kay," said Gerda to the river and, throwing her shoes into the water, she got into a boat which drifted away until at last it came to a strange, little house.

An old woman came out and Gerda told her about Kay. She took Gerda inside and gave her cherries to eat while she combed her hair with a magic comb to make her forget about Kay.

She wanted Gerda to stay as she had always wanted a little girl for her own. She charmed all the roses in the garden away in case they reminded Gerda of Kay. Sometimes Gerda thought she missed one particular flower but did not know which until she saw a rose painted on the old woman's hat and suddenly remembered Kay. She wept and where her tears fell a rose bush grew.

"He is not dead," the roses said.

"I must look for him," cried Gerda and set off without delay. Soon a big crow came and Gerda asked him if he had seen Kay.

"Perhaps, but surely he has forgotten you for the princess," said the crow and told of a princess who had promised to marry the man clever enough to make her laugh. All had failed till the arrival of a boy with a toboggan whose tales were wonderful and she had married him.

"Oh, will you take me there?" cried Gerda and the crow took her to a palace and showed her the princess's room. Gerda held her lamp and looked at the prince and called Kay's name. The prince awoke and sat up but it was not Kay. So she told her tale to the prince and princess and then fell asleep exhausted.

Next morning they gave Gerda fur-lined boots and a muff and a carriage to go and look for Kay. Gerda bade them farewell and the carriage rolled on through a forest until it was stopped by robbers. A woman drew out a big knife but, before she could hurt Gerda, her own daughter called out,

"She must play with me! She must give me her boots and her muff!"

That night Gerda stayed with the robbers. Wood-pigeons sat in the rafters above a reindeer tied to the wall. Gerda heard the pigeons coo,

"We have seen Kay. He was sitting in the sledge of the Snow Queen."

"Where did they go?" cried Gerda.

"To Finland," the pigeons said.

Next morning Gerda told the robber girl what the pigeons had said and she nodded and said,

"The reindeer will carry you to Finland."

Away it sped, running day and night. At last they reached Finland and stopped at a house. A woman let them in and they told her Kay's story.

"There is a splinter in Kay's heart," she said, "that must be removed or the Snow Queen will keep him for ever."

Kay had forgotten Gerda and his previous life and enjoyed living in the Snow Queen's castle but, when Gerda arrived, the Snow Queen was away and Kay was alone. Gerda knew him at once and kissed him and held him tight, crying,

"Kay, have I found you at last?"

Kay did not answer for his heart was frozen but then Gerda's tears fell on his chest and sank down into his heart and melted it. He recognised Gerda and burst into tears and his tears washed the speck of the magic mirror out of his eye.

"Gerda!" he cried. "At last!"

Gerda now wept for joy. Hand in hand they ran to the reindeer, waiting to take them home.

The roses were in bloom in the garden and Kay and Gerda knew they were really together again at last.

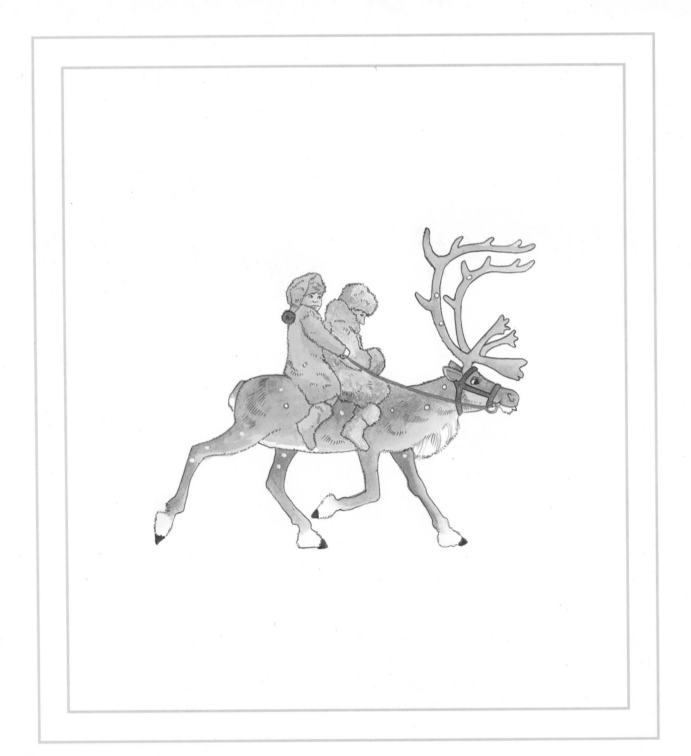

Thumbelina

Thumbelina

Once upon a time there was a woman who longed for a child. So desperate was she that she asked for help from a witch who gave her a seed and told her to watch what happened when she planted it in a flowerpot.

The plant grew and flowered and, when the bud opened, there, inside, was a tiny girl, no bigger than your thumb. The woman loved her dearly and called her Thumbelina.

Thumbelina's bed was a walnut shell with a rose-petal coverlet. She could row the walnut shell across a bowl of water using a pair of horsehairs as oars.

One night while Thumbelina was asleep in her walnut shell a hideous toad came clambering through the open window.

"What a pretty young girl. She would make a lovely bride for my son," the toad croaked to himself and, picking up the walnut shell with the sleeping Thumbelina inside, he hopped away.

When Thumbelina awoke she found herself on the leaf of a waterlily floating in the middle of a pond and the toad told her she was to marry his son.

She was horrified and burst into tears but the toads were pleased because toads cry only when they are happy.

A butterfly heard her sobs and used one of the horsehairs to tow the leaf to the bank while the toads were away. Thumbelina thanked her but before she could climb on to the bank a large stag beetle flew down, picked her up and carried her high into a tree. He thought she was beautiful and gave her a sweet flower to eat and paid her compliments.

However, when the other beetles came to see the new arrival they said she was ugly.

"Fancy," said one, "she has only two legs. How strange!"

"And no feelers at all!" added another. "She's very peculiar!"

In truth, Thumbelina was very beautiful but the stag beetle began to believe she was not and, deciding to let her go, he carried her to the ground and left her on a daisy.

As it was summer, Thumbelina could find food for herself and keep warm but when winter came she was very unhappy for the snow covered all her food and her clothes were too worn and ragged to be of any use.

She was sitting shivering one day when a fieldmouse found her and, taking pity on her, invited her into her warm, little house and took care of her.

Thumbelina was grateful to the little fieldmouse for saving her and spent many hours telling her stories. The old, blind mole used to listen too and, before long, he had fallen in love with her. He dug her a tunnel so that she could walk safely and one day Thumbelina found a swallow just inside the entrance. The mole thought he was dead but Thumbelina nursed him until he could fly away.

Soon the mole asked her to marry him and the fieldmouse told her how lucky she was. Thumbelina, however, did not want to live underground and never see the sun or the flowers again.

The mouse helped Thumbelina spin her trousseau and, just before the wedding, Thumbelina went. into the sunshine for the last time and asked the flowers to give the swallow her love if ever they saw him again.

Just then there came a joyous 'tweet' and the swallow was diving and swooping above her.

"Come with me! Come with me! I'll take you to my warm, summer lands and you can live there and be happy," sang the swallow.

So Thumbelina thanked the kind, little fieldmouse and asked her to explain to the old, blind mole that she could not live under the ground.

Then Thumbelina said goodbye to the flowers and climbed on the swallow's back. Up he flew, higher and higher, carrying her over fields and forests and then the deep blue of the sea. The air grew warmer as the swallow spiralled down towards some ruins; great tumbled pieces of stone with broken columns covered in greenery.

Thumbelina climbed down and looked round. From the flower trumpets jumped little people her own size.

"I am the Prince of the Flower Spirits," said one. "Welcome to our land."

Soon the Prince and Thumbelina fell in love and were married and lived happily ever after.

The Princess and The Pea

The Princess and The Pea

Long ago, in a far distant kingdom there lived a king and queen and their son. He was their only child and, from the day he was born, they gave him the very best of everything. He grew up tall and strong, a credit to his parents, and was clever, good-natured and handsome.

The prince began to think that it was time he found a girl to love and to marry. Of course, there were many young ladies from noble families who would have dearly loved to have become the prince's wife, but the queen told her son,

"When you marry, you must marry a TRUE princess. No-one else will be good enough."

The prince told his mother he would only consider young ladies who came from other royal families but even this did not satisfy the queen.

"They may come from royal families," she said, "but they may still not be TRUE princesses."

"How shall I be able to tell which young lady is a TRUE princess?" the prince wanted to know.

"Trust me, my son. I shall find you a TRUE princess to marry," said his mother.

The queen sent out messengers to make it known that the prince was looking for a princess. Those who wanted to be considered were to tell the palace. Each would be invited in turn to spend a night in the palace's guest suite. The royal family would then decide on the prince's bride.

The announcement also stated that only TRUE princesses would be considered.

The queen then gathered her servants to prepare the guest suite. In the bedroom was a large, comfortable bed with a soft, feather mattress but the queen ordered the puzzled servants to bring in nineteen more mattresses and to pile them, one on top of another, on to the guest bed.

With twenty mattresses on it, the bed was so high that a ladder was needed for anybody trying to get into it! Then, when no-one was looking, the queen slipped a single pea underneath the mattress that lay at the very bottom of the pile.

For the next few weeks a carriage would arrive every day with another hopeful lady. All of them tried to convince the queen that they were suitable.

As all claimed to be of royal birth they were asked careful questions to make sure that they were telling the truth. After dinner, each princess was then shown to the guest suite.

Some were beautiful, some were charming and most of them really did come from royal families. The prince spent time with each and some he liked very much but, according to the queen, none of them was a TRUE princess. In the morning she would ask each one the same question,

"Did you sleep well last night?"

Each girl would reply politely,

"Yes thank you, Ma'am, I slept very well."

Then the queen would frown and when the girl had left, she would turn to her son and say,

"She was not a TRUE princess. We must continue looking."

The prince was puzzled. How could the queen tell that none of them was a TRUE princess?

As time passed, the number of princesses coming to see the prince grew smaller and smaller and it began to seem as if they would never find a TRUE princess. Weeks went by and the prince began to feel sure he would never marry but the queen told him not to worry.

"Your princess will come one day. Wait and see!"

One dark and stormy night, the prince was feeling very gloomy when there was a knock on the door of the palace. The prince followed the servant who opened the door and he saw a very bedraggled young woman standing there.

"I am so cold and wet," she said. "May I stay here for the night until the storm dies down?"

He led her to a fireside chair and gave her hot food and wine. As she drank he could see her clothes were threadbare and she was barefoot.

"I was found in a forest far from here by a poor woman," the girl said. "She brought me up and tells me I am a princess from a distant kingdom."

She was beautiful and charming and the prince, wondering if she could be a TRUE princess, went to tell the queen.

The queen looked doubtful but said that of course she could stay for the night. The prince showed the girl to the guest suite and said goodnight, leaving her to climb the ladder to the top of the pile of mattresses.

Next morning, at breakfast, the girl looked even more tired than before. When the queen asked if she had slept well she hesitated and said,

"I hate to be rude, Ma'am, but I cannot lie. The bed was so lumpy I could not sleep a wink!"

"My son! At last we have found a TRUE princess!" the queen said delightedly.

The prince too was delighted but also puzzled.

"How do you know she is a TRUE princess?"

His mother took them both to the guest suite and took out the pea from under the mattress.

"Only a TRUE princess could feel *this* under twenty feather mattresses," she said.

The prince and princess laughed at the queen's craftiness and when he asked her to marry him she agreed and they went to make preparations for a great wedding celebration.

Pinocchio

Pinocchio

Once upon a time there was an old woodcarver called Geppetto. He was lonely and longed for a son so he decided to make himself a puppet for company. The Blue Fairy heard his wish and, when he had finished the carving, she made the puppet come to life. Geppetto was overjoyed and decided to call his new son Pinocchio.

However, Pinocchio was naughty, kicked his new father's shins and ran out into the street into the arms of a policeman. Poor Geppetto, for the policeman believed that he had beaten Pinocchio and took him to prison. So Pinocchio went back to the house where now he could do just as he liked.

After he had eaten he sat by the fire and a tiny cricket warned him,

"Beware! Boys who don't listen to their fathers are always sorry later." Naughty Pinocchio ignored this advice.

When Geppetto came back he found Pinocchio asleep so close to the fire that his wooden feet had burned away. Geppetto made some more and told him he must go to school like a real boy but he was so poor he had to sell his coat to buy Pinocchio a spelling book and some clothes.

Pinocchio was sorry and said he would be a good boy at school but, on the way there, he heard some music and went to see what was happening.

The music was from a travelling puppet show and Pinocchio was thrilled to see puppets, just like himself, on the stage and hurried to join them. It was a disaster, for the other puppets had long strings and he soon became entangled.

The puppet master was furious and threatened to throw him on the fire as fuel but when Pinocchio begged for his life the puppet master relented.

"I'll throw Harlequin on instead."

"No! No!" cried Pinocchio. "It's not his fault. Burn me after all."

He was touched by Pinocchio's bravery and gave him some gold coins as a reward to take home to Geppetto.

Someone saw Pinocchio's money!

Going home to give the money to Geppetto he met the thieving cat and fox who had seen him get the money but clever Pinocchio hid it from the wicked pair in his shoe. They were angry and left him tied to the branch of a tree.

Now, the Blue Fairy had been watching over Pinocchio all this time and she rescued him and asked him about the money. He lied and said he had lost it. As he lied his nose grew longer and longer. The Blue Fairy laughed and said,

'That's what will always happen when you tell lies, Pinocchio!"

"I'm sorry! I'll be good!" he cried.

So she called some woodpeckers to peck his nose back to its right size.

Pinocchio promised to tell the truth and set off again for home. He really did mean to be good but, alas, he met a naughty boy who told him about a place called Toyland.

"There's no school, no rules to keep and lollipops grow on trees there!"

Pinocchio had a wonderful time at first but having fun all day and not doing any work was very bad for him, and all the other boys, and, bit by bit, they found they were all turning into donkeys with furry ears. Pinocchio was sold to a circus and made to do tricks. When he fell and hurt his leg and could no longer work, the cruel ringmaster threw him over a cliff into the sea.

As soon as Pinocchio fell into the water the magic spell from Toyland was broken and he was once more a puppet.

While he was floating in the sea he thought how sorry he was for all his naughty deeds and he was afraid that he would never see Geppetto again.

Suddenly he was swallowed by a huge fish. Poor Pinocchio was terrified for he could see nothing in the darkness. When he could stand he saw a tiny light and walked towards it.

Wonder of wonders! It was a little fire built by Geppetto who had been swallowed by the very same fish when he had been sailing and searching for his lost Pinocchio.

Joyfully they hugged each other and then Geppetto said tearfully,

"Oh, Pinocchio, now we are both marooned in this terrible place."

"Don't worry, Father. We'll think of something," said Pinocchio bravely. "I know! Let's build the fire bigger and see what happens."

So they did until all the smoke made the fish sneeze and, with his third sneeze, out they shot on to a beach and there was the Blue Fairy, waiting for them.

"Pinocchio, this is your reward for saving Geppetto's life."

Pinocchio became a real boy and he and Geppetto lived happily ever after.

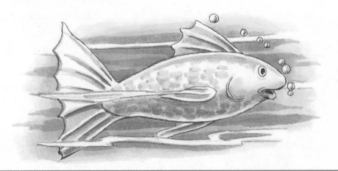

Goldilocks and the Three Bears

Goldilocks and the Three Bears

Once upon a time there was a little girl called Goldilocks. She had been given that name because her hair shone like gold in the sun.

Her mother had warned her not to wander into the great forest which lay close to their cottage, for fear she would get lost, but Goldilocks did not always do as she was told and, one day when she was bored with all her toys, she made sure her mother was not watching and ran quickly down the path into the great forest, certain that she would be able to find her way home.

She wandered happily in the forest looking at all the birds and flowers and once she saw some rabbits playing. When she was tired she decided to go home but, on turning round, she found the paths looked very different and could not find the right one. She soon realised she was lost and did not even know in which direction her home lay.

"Oh, I wish I had listened to Mother;' she said as she sank down on a log and burst into tears.

Bravely, she dried her tears and, when she had walked a little further, saw a tiny cottage among the trees.

Goldilocks crept towards the cottage, knocked on the door and peeped in the windows but no-one came. She pushed the front door and it opened.

"What a pretty cottage," thought Goldilocks and saw that there were three bowls of porridge on the table-a big one, a middle-sized one and a small one.

She was hungry by this time and tried the big bowl but that was too hot. She tried the middle-sized bowl but that was too cold. She tried the small bowl and that was just right and before she knew what she had done she had eaten it all up.

By the fire were three chairs, a big one, a middle-sized one and small one. Goldilocks tried the big chair but that was too high. She tried the middle-sized one but that was too hard. When she tried the small one that was just right but it broke as she sat down.

Then she saw the staircase. Upstairs were three beds — a big one, a middle-sized one and a small one. Goldilocks tried the big bed but that was too hard. She tried the middle-sized one but that was too soft. The small one was just right and soon she was fast asleep.

The cottage belonged to three bears and when they returned Father Bear growled in his big, loud voice,

"Who has been tasting my porridge?"

"Who has been tasting my porridge?" said Mother Bear in her soft, gentle voice.

"Who has eaten all my porridge up and left me none at all?" cried Baby Bear in his squeaky, little voice.

Then Father Bear saw his chair and growled in his big, loud voice,

"Who has been sitting in my chair?"

"Who has been sitting in my chair?" said Mother Bear in her soft, gentle voice.

"And who has been sitting in my chair and broken it all to pieces?" cried Baby Bear in his squeaky, little voice.

Father Bear said in his big, loud voice,

"Look, there are muddy footprints on the floor leading upstairs."

So the three bears followed the footprints up the stairs.

"Who has been sleeping in my bed?" growled Father Bear in his big, loud voice.

"Who has been sleeping in my bed?" said Mother Bear in her soft, gentle voice.

"Who has been sleeping in my bed and is still there, fast asleep?" cried Baby Bear in his squeaky, little voice.

Astonished, the three bears all looked at Baby Bear's bed where, fast asleep, lay Goldilocks with her golden hair spread across the pillow.

291

"She ate all my porridge and she broke my chair," wailed Baby Bear.

Goldilocks was dreaming and the voices from downstairs had become part of her dream but Baby Bear's squeaky, little voice in her ear woke her up and she sat up rubbing her eyes.

"Oh, my!" she screamed and, jumping out of bed, ran across the bedroom, down the stairs and out of the door before the bears could move.

She ran and ran, down the path, across the clearing and into the woods, until she came to her own little cottage.

Goldilocks never went wandering in the great forest again.